W9-BPL-983

Disney
MⓄANA

Spirit of Adventure

MOANA1190583

Code is valid for your Disney Moana ebook and may be redeemed through the Disney Story Central
app on the App Store. Content subject to availability. Parent permission required.
Code expires on December 31, 2019.

PaRragon

Bath · New York · Cologne · Melbourne · Delhi
Hong Kong · Shenzhen · Singapore

M[...] on the beautiful island of Motunui.
She loves the ocean.

Chief Tui is Moana's father. He is also the ██████ of Motunui.

Chief Tui e leads [...] to the top of Motunui's highest mountain.

He wants Moana to take over as chief someday.

go back
to

If you lived on an island, what would it look like?
Design and color in your island below.

Baby Moana is collecting pretty flowers on the beach.
Draw lines to link the matching pairs. Can you spot one
flower without a pair? When you do, circle it!

Answers on page 95

7

This is Moana's Gramma Tala. She is very wise, and she understands Moana's love of the ocean.

When Moana was little, Gramma Tala would tell stories to the village children about the demigod, Maui, and the mother island, Te Fiti.

Maui was a trickster. He stole the heart of Te Fiti,
and darkness spread across the land!

Moana loved to hear Tala's stories about Te Fiti, Maui, and the ocean, even though the other children found them a little scary!

Draw a line from the close-ups below
to where they belong in the big picture.

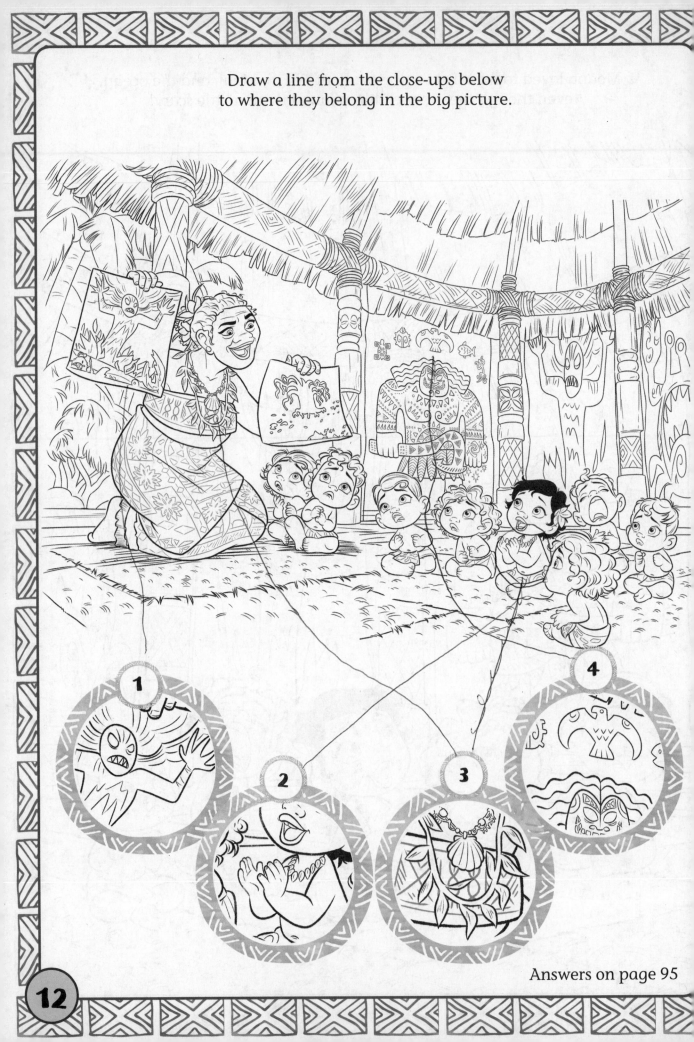

Answers on page 95

Match up the pieces to complete the picture of Moana
rescuing a baby turtle from the hungry birds.

One day, Moana was playing by the beach. She helped a baby turtle make its way back into the ocean and away from some hungry birds.

The baby turtle joined its mother in the ocean.

Moana watched as the waves pulled back and forth,
and something washed up on the beach.

The ocean had given Moana a gift—a beautiful conch shell.

17

Suddenly, the ocean parted and formed a magical canyon of water.
Moana reached in and grasped a stone. It was the heart of Te Fiti!

Moana loved growing up on Motunui and living by the ocean.

19

Match up the pieces to complete the picture
of Moana and the heart of Te Fiti.

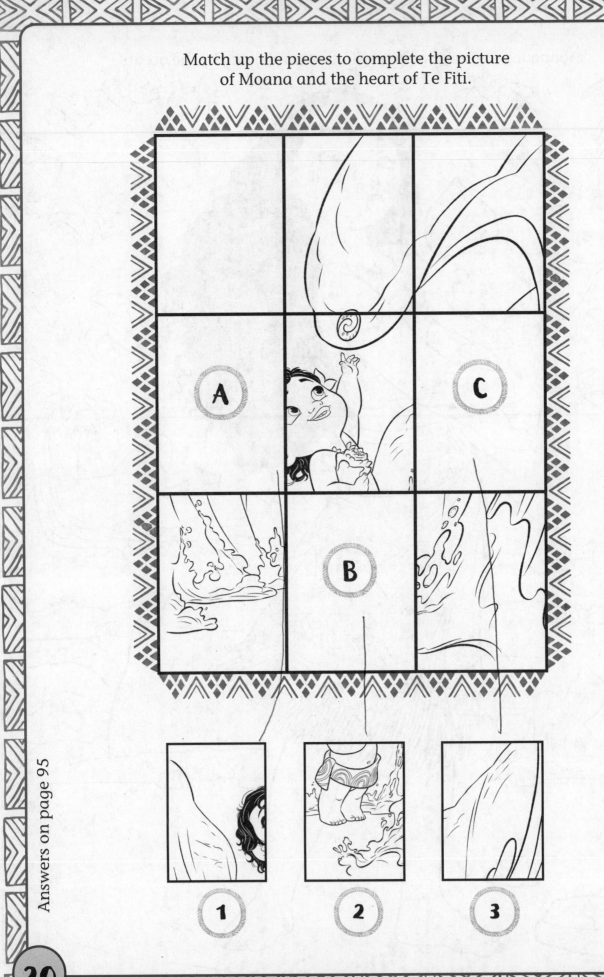

There are five differences between these two pictures of Maui.
Can you spot them? Color in a flower below each time you find one.

Answers on page 95

21

Pua is Moana's lovable pet pig. He would do anything for Moana!

Heihei is the village rooster. He's always making silly mistakes!

One day, Gramma Tala takes Moana to the cavern of her ancestors.

Moana discovers that her ancestors were ocean voyagers!

Who is Heihei looking at? Connect the dots to
reveal the lovable animal, then color in the picture.

Color in the shapes with the dots to reveal Moana's loyal friends.

Gramma Tala thinks Moana should sail beyond the reef,
find Maui, and return the heart of Te Fiti.

Gramma Tala becomes very ill. Before she passes away,
she gives Moana her special necklace to bring her luck.

Moana borrows a boat from the cavern
of her ancestors and prepares to set sail.

But when Moana and Heihei are out on the ocean,
they get caught in a terrible storm.

Help Moana and Heihei sail their way through
the wavy maze and out of the storm.

Start

Finish

Answer on page 95

What does Moana learn about her ancestors?
Use the code below to fill in the letters and reveal the answer.

W E

W E R E

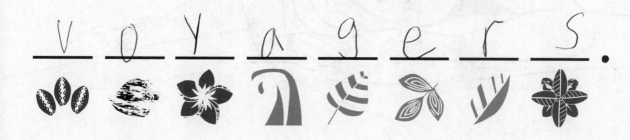

V O Y A G E R S.

Answer on page 95

33

After the storm, Moana and Heihei find themselves shipwrecked on a distant island. It's Maui's island!

Maui is a demigod of wind and sea. He once had a magical fishhook that helped him shape-shift into different animals, but he lost it in a battle with Te Kā.

Maui has lots of amazing tattoos—some of them even come to life!
This tattoo is called Mini-Maui. He keeps Maui in line.

Moana wants Maui to help her restore Te Fiti's heart, but he just wants to find his fishhook. Maui steals Moana's canoe, but the ocean picks her up and puts her back on the boat!

The tattoos that cover Maui's body tell stories of his adventures.
Use your imagination to write a story about the tattoo below.

Maui has stolen Moana's canoe! Help her get it back by
following the path of canoes through the grid to Maui.
Move only forward, backward, up, and down—not diagonally.

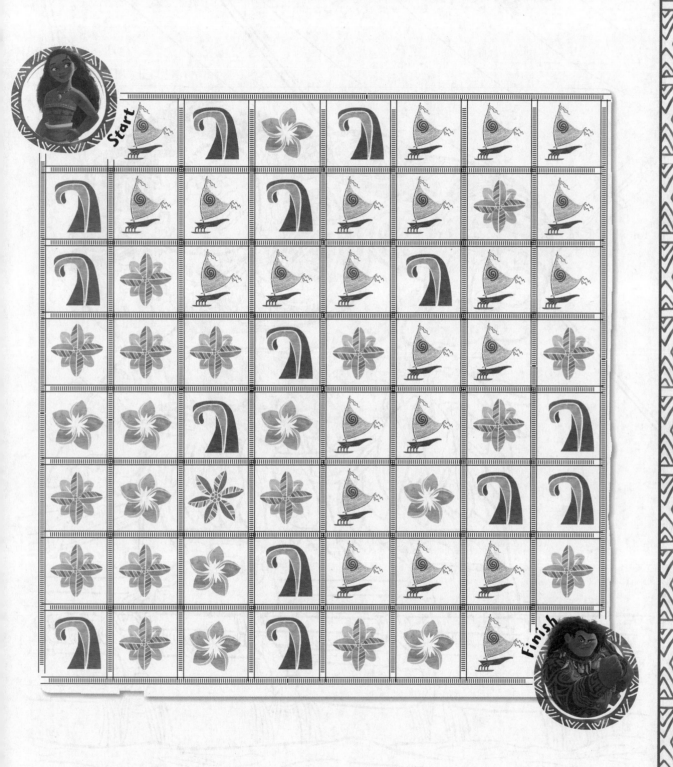

Answer on page 95

Maui is shocked to see the ocean bring Moana
back to the canoe. He can't escape her that easily!

The Kakamora live nearby. They sail out to see what is happening.

The Kakamora are little creatures with coconut armor.
They paint angry faces on their shells.

The chief of the Kakamora decides to attack Moana and Maui.

Beware the Kakamora! Draw an angry face
on each of the coconut pirates below.

Draw a line between each of the Kakamora and their matching shadows.

1

2

3

4

A

B

C

D

Answers on page 96

Just as the Kakamora jump on Moana's canoe,
Heihei swallows the heart of Te Fiti.

The Kakamora then decide to steal Heihei!

Maui shows Moana how to scare away the Kakamora.
He makes a warrior face.

Moana practices her warrior face. She looks fierce!

Help Moana rescue Heihei from the Kakamora
by finding the path that leads to him.

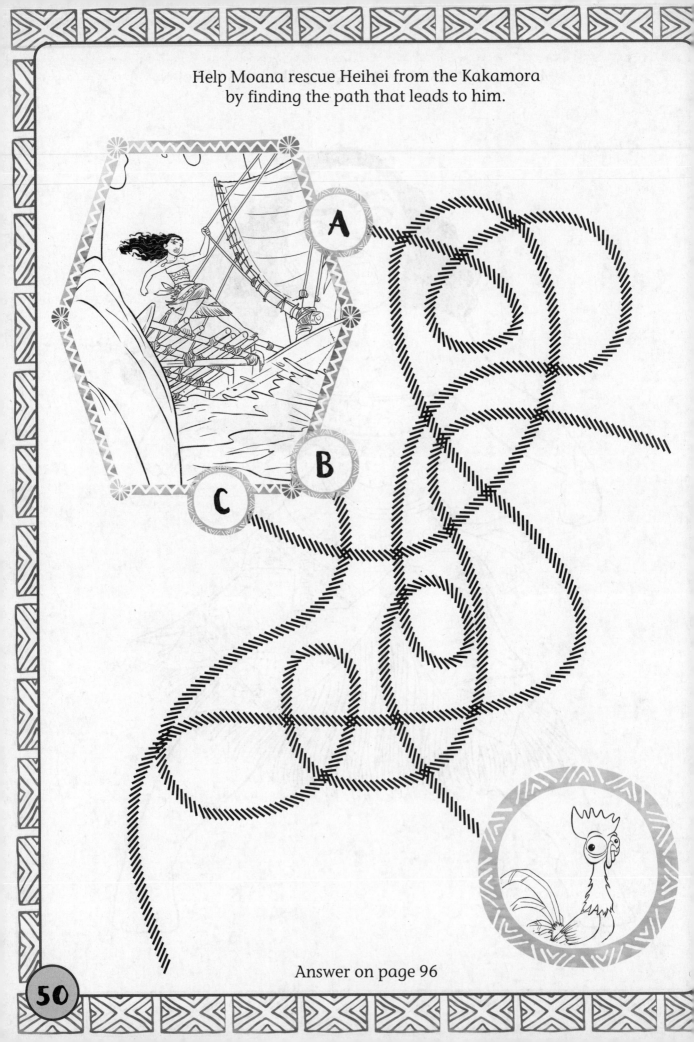

Answer on page 96

The Kakamora are trying to trick you! Can you outsmart them?
Find the creatures that appear twice, and then color them in!

Answers on page 96

Moana rescues Heihei just before he's handed to
the chief of the Kakamora, and they make their escape.

Moana paddles away as quickly as she can.

Moana listens as Maui tells her about his stolen fishhook.
He really wants to get it back.

Maui agrees to help Moana restore Te Fiti's heart on one condition: she must help him find his magical fishhook first. They travel to Lalotai, the realm of monsters.

Moana, Maui, and Pua are practicing their warrior poses.
Match each picture to its close-up.

Answers on page 96

Look carefully at the pictures of the mischievous coconut creatures.
Match each picture to its close-up.

Answers on page 96

Maui's fishhook had been stolen by Tamatoa, a giant treasure-collecting crab. He doesn't want to return it.

Maui spots his fishhook and grabs it, making Tamatoa very angry!

Moana jumps in front of Maui and scares Tamatoa with her warrior face.

Together, Moana and Maui flee Tamatoa and escape the realm of monsters.

These pictures of Maui may look the same, but one is different.
Can you spot which one?

Answer on page 96

Moana and Maui meet lots of monsters in Lalotai.
Draw your own monster below and color it in.

Don't forget to give the monster a name:

....

Moana and Maui get back to the canoe safely.
Maui is happy to have his magical fishhook back.

Maui tries to shape-shift using his fishhook . . .
but it doesn't seem to be working!

Soon, Moana and Maui come face-to-face with Te Kā—
a huge, angry monster of hot lava and orange fire.

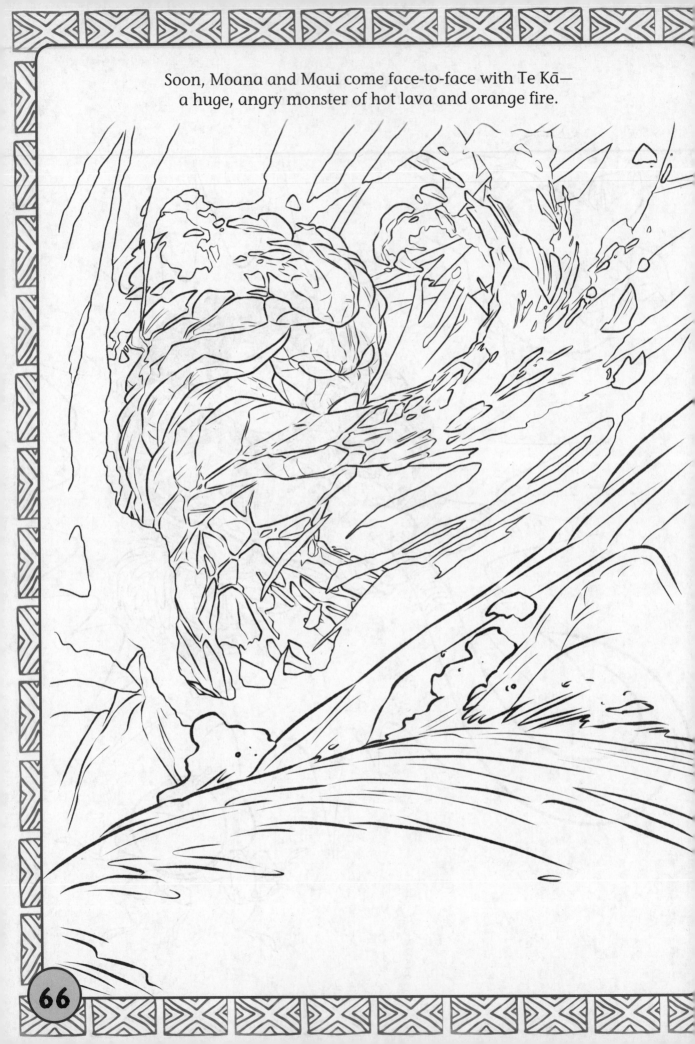

Maui and Te Kā fight, and Te Kā's fist cracks Maui's fishhook.

Maui can shape-shift into lots of different animals. If you could shape-shift like Maui, what kind of animal would you become? Draw it below.

Spot and circle four differences in the lower picture of Maui, then color it in!

Answers on page 96

Maui feels sad and defeated. He shape-shifts into a hawk and flies away, leaving Moana alone.

Moana is ready to give up. She throws the heart of Te Fiti into the ocean.

Suddenly, Moana sees a huge manta ray in the water.

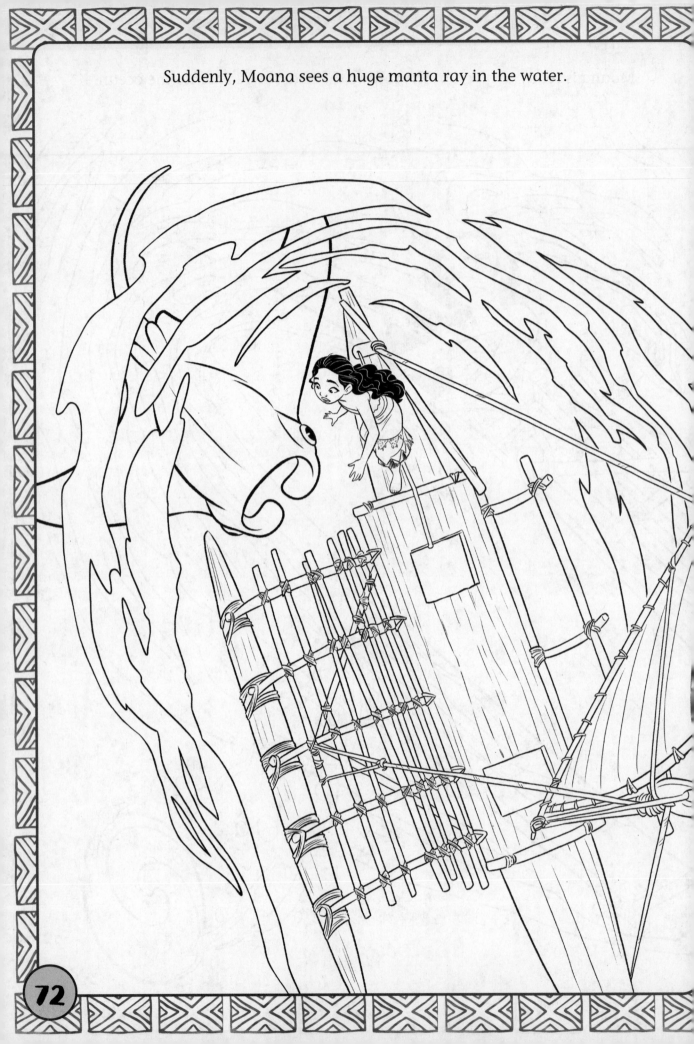

The spirit of Gramma Tala appears on Moana's canoe. Suddenly, Moana is surrounded by the boats of her ancestors, who sing a song to give her comfort.

The spirit of Gramma Tala has a message for Moana.
Write down every second letter to reveal the message.

laklhwmagycs
qkpnrogw
twjhaotyiohu
fabrde

_ _ _ _ _ _
_ _ _ _   _ _ _
_ _ _   _ _ _.

Answer on page 96

Moana spots a magical manta ray racing toward her.
Which path leads the manta ray to the canoe?

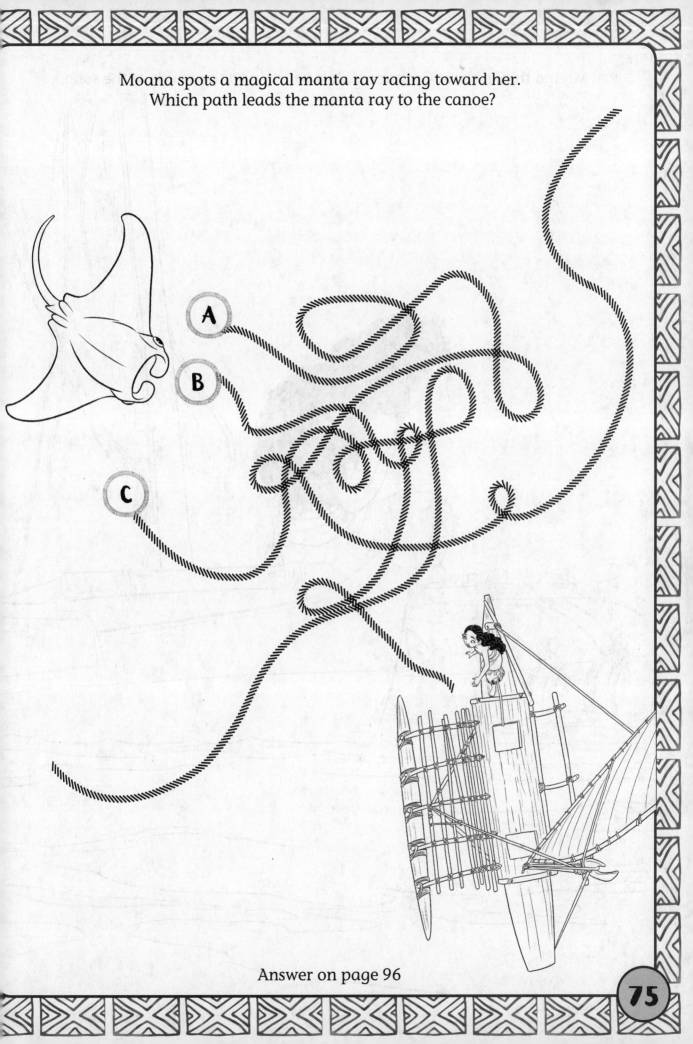

Answer on page 96

Moana thinks about Gramma Tala's words, and the words of the song.

Moana is inspired to go on. She dives into the ocean and picks up the heart of Te Fiti from the ocean floor.

Moana fixes her boat and prepares to set sail once more.

Moana is ready. She bravely travels toward Te Fiti.

Maui has shape-shifted into a hawk. Can you spot
which shadow exactly matches Maui?

Answer on page 96

Connect the dots to complete the picture of the lava monster, Te Kā.

Moana must use her expert sailing skills
to get past Te Kā if she is to reach Te Fiti.

Just then, Maui returns! He won't let Moana face Te Kā alone.

While Maui battles Te Kā, Moana races toward Te Fiti.

Te Kā knocks down Maui and breaks his magical fishhook.

Moana reaches Te Fiti, which is now just a hollow shell. She holds up the glowing heart and sings the song of her ancestors to Te Kā.

Moana offers the heart of Te Fiti to Te Kā.
Just then, the face of the lava monster transforms to reveal . . .

. . . Te Fiti! Te Fiti had become Te Kā when her heart was stolen! Te Fiti smiles and returns Maui's hook. The island explodes with flowers and comes back to life at last.

Together, Maui and Moana have defeated Te Kā
and restored Te Fiti's heart. Now, the friends hug good-bye.

Imagine you are going on an ocean adventure like Moana,
and design and draw your own boat below.

While Moana has been gone, her father, Chief Tui, has been trying to find her! Can you help him through the maze to Moana?

Start

Finish

Answer on page 96

With his hook, Maui shape-shifts into a hawk and prepares to fly away.

Moana waves good-bye to her friend Maui. Moana's people are voyagers once again, and she is ready to lead them out onto the ocean.

Decorate the island of Te Fiti by drawing trees, plants, and flowers.
Don't forget to show the sun shining!

Answers

Page 7

Page 21

Page 12

Page 32

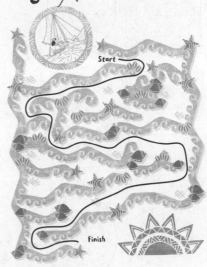

Page 33

WE WERE VOYAGERS.

Page 13

1–B 2–D
3–A 4–C

Page 20

1–A 2–B
3–C

Page 39

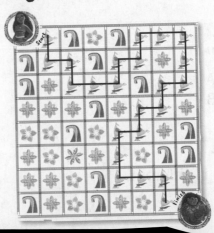

Answers

Page 45
1–B   2–C
3–D   4–A

Page 50
Path A

Page 51

Page 56
1–B   2–C
3–A

Page 57
1–D   2–A
3–C   4–B

Page 62
Picture D is different.

Page 69

Page 74
Always know who you are.

Page 75
Path B

Page 80
Shadow C

Page 91